Dear Mothership,

Alert the Federation—I believe that my latest report, *Trash Crisis on Earth*, has fallen into the hands of the mini-brains!

I can only hope that they will be unable to comprehend its true meaning. Perhaps they will believe it to be simply the product of a gifted Earth child's overactive imagination.

If, and I doubt that it will come to this, my true identity is revealed, I am fully prepared to face the consequences. As you know, Mothership, I fear nothing.

Your Faithful Agent,

Julian Rodriguez
Federation Officer, First Rank

JULIAN RODRIGUEZ
EPISODE ONE

TRASH CRISIS ON EARTH

Alexander Stadler

This book was brought to you by
Andrew Baker, Kara LaReau, and
Holly McGhee.

Outrageous!

OUTRAGEOUS!

That is the only word that can possibly describe the treatment I have received on this pathetic little planet!

Mothership, you sent me here to study the ways of these mini-brained Earthlings and I accepted your "undercover mission" against my better judgment.

I am an officer of the Federation and I know that it is my duty to go where I am most needed.

For eight long years, I have been disguised as an Earth juvenile.

I have never complained, despite the mistreatment, deprivation, insults, and disrespect I have endured at the hands of these primitive life-forms.

Rise and shine, Mr. Spaceman!

EXHIBIT A

Why would you spray paint the bathtub

EXHIBIT B

I have faithfully reported back
to you about their ridiculous
culture, their pointless comings
and goings, their nonsensical
sayings and doings.

I have done it gladly because I
live to serve the Federation and
to serve YOU, Mothership.

But this is the last straw!

Today I was treated in a way
that could only be categorized as

HUMILIATING!

UTTERLY **HUMILIATING!**

Mothership:

Say it isn't so,
Officer Rodriguez!
One who has seen battle
in the farthest reaches
of unknown space,
a hero known throughout
the galaxy for his bravery
as well as his undeniable charm,
First Officer Julian Rodriguez
has been humiliated?
We find that hard to believe.

By the honor of the Federation, Mothership, I swear that every word I report to you is factually based.

Mothership:

*Officer,
please describe the situation
in greater detail.
We are having difficulty
comprehending how
THE Julian Rodriguez
could have been so
utterly disgraced.*

I will describe the events exactly as they occurred, Mothership.

You will discover how I have suffered at the hands of these evil Earthlings.

You will see what a **torture** this existence amongst the mini-brains can be.

You will know the **injustices** that have been committed against me, and you will be **horrified**.

HORRIFIED!

Mothership:

*The mainframe
is prepared for your transmission,
First Officer Rodriguez.
Commence uploading.*

Very well.
It began
early
this
morning
at 0700
hours
when
The
Paternal
Unit
disrupted
my
sleep
state,

fed me a substance I can only
describe as intergalactic space
sludge,

and presented me with my midday
nutrition capsule.

   With this lunch in hand I was
sent off to the education center.

As you know, Mothership, I have strict dietary requirements. I must consume significant quantities of salts, fats, and sugars.

Without these vital resources I cannot be expected to survive in this toxic atmosphere.

I have informed The Paternal Unit over and over again that my noontime capsule is an important part of my regimen.

It must contain

energy-rich sponge cake

protective chocolate coating

wholesome creme-filled center

1. At least two portions of the Earth food known as Ring Ding;

jam-packed with nutrients (heavenly nectar-like taste) and antigravitational properties

2. A delicious liquid energy source known as Strawberry Fizz; and

3. One hermetically sealed packet of Cool Ranch Krispy Poofs.

Krispy Poofs

sealed for ultimate freshness

practically weightless (important during space travel)

Well, Mothership, despite
my repeated entreaties and
explanations, this morning I was
once again presented with

1. Some woodlike
sticks of something
called carrot;

useless → flavor-deprived

2. A flavorless
transparent liquid
called water,
which tastes like
nothing at all; and

invisible, hydrating, yes, but otherwise utterly useless, with none of the extraordinary benefits of Strawberry Fizz

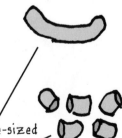

3. Something called
a veggie-dog, which is
too disgusting for me
to even put into words.

veggie-dog cut into bite-sized but still-repulsive pieces

I disposed of these noxious
materials at my earliest
opportunity.

Once again I managed to pass
unscathed from my home study site
to the education center.

I have succeeded in befriending
a foot-traffic controller who
facilitates my entrances and exits
to and from the location.

Mothership:

Ahh, the education center.
We know that you have
learned much of Earth ``culture``
there in the past.

Indeed. As you know, it has been a challenge for me to conceal my natural intellectual superiority from the mini-brains.

For the most part I have been successful. But today I was tested in a way that would have challenged the abilities of even the strongest grade-six warrior.

Mothership:

Great Voltron!
What have you endured?

At the start of the day it was announced over their crude information deployment system that all normal daily programming had been canceled.

I and all of my mini-brained companions were to be subjected to a six-hour marathon of something called
STATE ASSESSMENT TESTS.

Mothership:

*We are not sure
we understand.
Can you explain for us
the meaning of
"State Assessment Tests"?*

Do you recall the reports
I submitted after my life-
threatening mission to the medical
pavilion, where I suffered at the
hands of the evil Dr. Zimmerman
and his killer nursebot?

Mothership:

Of course,
First Officer Rodriguez,
every member of the Federation
is aware of the bravery
you exhibited there
in the face of
mind-bending pain.

Well, this was very much like that.

I was herded into a steamy, airless mess hall with hundreds of the poor little mini-brains.

ARETHA FRANKLIN ELEMENTARY

The shades were drawn so that we could not see the light of day.

For hours, we were made to fill in small circles with a clumsy stick of wood and graphite.

Page after page of soul-numbing
questions involving trains and
miles per hour were placed in
front of us.

For what seemed like a millennium my mind was held in the vicelike grip of a concept known as GREATER THAN/LESS THAN.

At the middle section of the
day we were briefly released to
restore our strength with our
nutrition capsules.

I, as you know, had none.

Then it was right back to the tests.
Imagine a great mind like mine
being forced to struggle with this
petty minutiae!

I, Julian Rodriguez, who comprehends

multiplication in all its complex
majesty, was made to toil with
concepts that any standard
Federation infant would have
mastered by the age of three!

49

Mothership:

Inconceivable.
This sounds worse
than the ritual water torture
they call "Bath Time"!
How did you withstand it,
First Officer?

I will never know, Mothership, I will never know.

By the luck of the universe, just when I was on the verge of breaking down, an alarm signal blared and we were all released.

ARETHA FRANKLIN ELEMENTARY

Weak from hunger, I made my way
back to my home study site.

On the way there I was ambushed by
alien mercenaries —

the villainess Mamie and her
henchwoman, Doris. You may recall
them from my report on Stardate 19,
titled **Girlattack**.

I suspect that they were after my dat

ank, but they were no match for me.

I quickly subdued them with a wave

of my cubic zirconian light saber

and escaped their
clutches with the
documents intact.

I know what you are thinking,
Mothership. What I have described
should be no match for a four-
times-decorated Federation
officer.

And you are right to
think it. I have faced
far worse terrors in
my illustrious career.

However, my trials were far from over. I was about to confront the greatest injustice of all.

All at the hands of · · ·

Evilomami.

Mothership:

Evilomami?

Perhaps you remember her from my past reports.

She is the supervisor of my home study site.

all-seeing eyes

energy source

communication device

You may have heard me refer to her as The Maternal Unit.

Mothership:

Ah yes, Evilomami,
the cruel supervisor
who thwarts you at every turn.
What difficulties
did she present on this
particular occasion?

As I said before, she has
humiliated me.

Mothership:

But how,
First Officer Rodriguez?
How?

Starving, dehydrated, and very possibly near death, I returned to the home study site.

When I entered the domicile, Evilomami was present but paid me little attention. She was, as usual, chattering away on her primitive communication device.

I had hoped to be offered a small bit of food upon my return. I received nothing.

With no one to turn to, I attempted to prepare a small snack for myself.

The Earthlings have a strange ritual regarding their eating habits. In the afternoons, they practice a form of fasting known as saving your appetite.

You know
you're not supposed
to have any snacks
before dinner.

It is a very cruel custom and
one which, I believe, causes much
of the discord on this troubled
planet.

Hmmm . . .
I must have
forgotten.

Despite my efforts, my snack was confiscated. Evilomami left me with an allegedly nutritious spheroid.

It met the same fate as my
so-called lunch.

Then, Mothership, I was assigned hard labor.

The Maternal Unit insisted that I dispose of a large canister, filled to the brim with humanoid refuse!

This was not work fit for an officer of the Federation! Oh no! Even when I was a lowly day-camp apprentoid I was never asked to perform such chores.

Not since the Great Cafeteria Rebellion have I seen such filth. It brought to mind the words of the poet Silverstein:

"And so it piled up to the ceilings:
Coffee grounds, potato peelings,
Brown bananas, rotten peas,
Chunks of sour cottage cheese."

And the odor!

Mothership:

Was it unbearable?

I am, as you know, a brave
explorer and I have experienced my
fair share of horrors throughout
the known and unknown universe.

But that refuse pile was unlike anything I have ever seen or smelled.

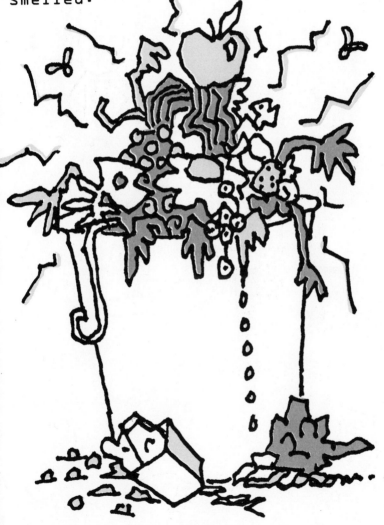

Mothership:

For our records,
Rodriguez,
could the stench level
be quantified?

The reek was worse than the
breath of that mini-brain they
call Stinky Weinbaum.

Knowing that the fumes might well knock me unconscious, I tried to buy some time by restoring my energy in front of the V-MER (Viewing Monitor for Entertainment and Relaxation).

I have found this device to be an invaluable research tool. Ever a servant to the Federation, I had been hoping to devote what remained of my afternoon to studying it in depth.

Evilomami seemed unaware of my fragile condition and demanded once again that I remove the stinking waste.

I clearly explained to my tormentor that I was in need of at least fifteen more minutes of rest and that without it I might very well collapse.

Half an hour later, just as my strength was beginning to return, Evilomami reappeared.

Perhaps, at that moment, I could have performed the revolting task. But during the brief time I had been studying the V-MER, I had become engrossed in a fascinating earthly form of programming known as cartoons.

Oh, these cartoons, Mothership!
You really must allow me to
upload a few into your mainframe.
They are quite extraordinary!

Although primitive, they contain action, danger, suspense, and humor—anything and everything a citizen of the universe might need to know.

Evilomami has no understanding of the value of these cartoons. I have heard her say on several occasions that she considers them to be mindless trash.

And trash was certainly what
she had on her mind when she once
again interrupted me, this time
with fury in her eyes.

Mothership, she treated me like a lowly minion! Without even saying please, she demanded that I deactivate the V-MER that very instant and take the stenchy mess to its disposal station.

And then she threatened me! She threatened me with imprisonment!

NO. We're not waiting for the "good part." There is no good part. You are going to your room RIGHT NOW, JULIAN EMANUEL RODRIGUEZ, and you are not coming out until you are ready to TAKE OUT THIS TRASH!!!

As you know, Mothership, I am not one to suffer threats.

And that,
Mothership,
is why I now
find myself
languishing
in this
earthly
prison.

They have tried to break me, but
my pride is intact.

Mothership:

*Officer Rodriguez,
this is indeed
as shocking a report
as you have ever transmitted.
Truly, I am dismayed
by your ordeal.*

Mothership:

On another note,
First Officer, may I ask
what that strange rumbling is
that I detect in the vicinity
of your transmitter?

That, Mothership, is the sound
of my deprived digestive system.
These heartless Earthlings
are attempting to starve me into
submission. Until I give in to
their demands, I am to be denied
all forms of nutrition.

Mothership:

*But this is too much!
It is an affront
to the entire Federation!
It is torture
of the lowest order!
It cannot be permitted!
First Officer Rodruguez,
prepare to be beamed
aboard!*

*We are
removing you
from this situation
immediately.
Beings which engage
in this kind of
behavior cannot be
allowed to
exist.*

Yes, Mothership!

Release me from this earthly prison!

Mothership:

Very well, First Officer.
Prepare for
Molecular Transmission.
As soon as you
are safely on board
we will set our tasers to
ANNIHILATE
and blow their whole planet
to smithereens.

Mothership:

*What is it,
Rodriguez?*

I cannot let this happen!

Forgive them, Mothership! They know not what they do!

The Earthlings' brains are limited, and they certainly can be very nasty. But surely they do not deserve to be destroyed!

Mothership:

But what other option is there?
An officer of the Federation
cannot be left to starve.

Mothership, if it will save the lives of these poor wretches, I will make the ultimate sacrifice.

Mothership:

You mean, you will . . .

Yes.

Yes.

I will remove the refuse.

Mothership:

Very well, Rodriguez.
You must do as you see fit.
We will comply with your wishes.
After all, you understand
these Earthlings
far better than
we ever will.

Thank you, Mothership.
And now, I must sign off.
Duty calls!
All hail the Federation!

Mothership:

*All hail the Federation,
Officer Rodriguez!
We await your
next transmission!*

123

LIBRARY OF CONGRESS CATALOGING-IN-PUBLICATION DATA AVAILABLE

ISBN-13: 978-0-439-91966-1
ISBN-10: 0-439-91966-5

10 9 8 7 6 5 4 3 2 1   08 09 10 11

Printed in the U.S.A.   23
First edition, May 2008

The author would like to extend a big outer space
thank-you to

Carla Caruso; Emily van Beek; Maryann Connolly;
Barbara Carter; The Eisenberg Solloway Family;
Dr. Ruth Greenberg; Elena Sisto; Brian Selznick;
Josephine Albarelli; Heidi Bleacher; Chris Bartlett;
Steve Scott; Carol Sue Steinbach; Henry M. Stadler;
Lily G. Stadler; Dr. Jean Baker; Jane Brodie;
Joan Stevens and That Ugly Baby; Darrin Britting;
Dr. Carl Berger; Betty Sorace and the staff at
Can Do! Copies in Philadelphia; Kerry Coleman;
my parents, John and Charlotte Stadler;
The Family of Henry and Josie; Marcy Hermsader;
Simon Brodie Buonacalza; and Mr. Julian Carter.

This book was art directed,
designed, and typeset by
Marijka Kostiw. It was
edited by Kara LaReau.
The jacket and interior
art was created using pen
and ink on paper. The
interior art was digitally
colored by Jonathan Luciano
and Alexander Stadler.
The jacket display type
was hand lettered by
Alexander Stadler. The
jacket type and background
were colored and styled by
Marc Tauss.

The text type was set
in OCR-A, a font created in
1968 by the American Type
Founders. The interior
type for the Mothership was
set in Break, a GarageFont.
The voice bubble and
label type were set in
Schmalex2000, a font custom
created from Alex Stadler's
own hand lettering.

Production of this book
was supervised by Joy
Simpkins, and manufacturing
was supervised by Jess
White. The book was
printed and bound at
R. R. Donnelly.